THE ALICE AND JERRY BASIC READERS
READING FOUNDATION PROGRAM

The New DAY IN AND DAY OUT

by
MABEL O'DONNELL

illustrators
FLORENCE J. HOOPES
MARGARET C. HOOPES

ROW, PETERSON & COMPANY
HOME OFFICE: EVANSTON, ILLINOIS

CONTENTS

ALICE and JERRY

SURPRISE

3192

ANIMALS

BETSY LEE

MR. CARL and JACK

GOOD NIGHT

ALICE and JERRY

Little Rabbit

"Alice, Alice!" said Jerry.
"Come here! Come here!
I see something brown."

Alice looked down.

She saw something little.

She saw something brown.

She saw a little brown rabbit.

"Oh, look, Jerry," said Alice.

Little Rabbit saw Jerry.

She saw Alice, too.

Hop went the rabbit.

Hop, hop, hop!

Alice and Jerry ran and ran.

Little Rabbit saw something.

She saw a hole.

A little brown rabbit hole!

Down, down she went.

"Oh!" said Alice and Jerry.

Toys

Jerry saw toys and toys and toys.

"Oh, Father," said Jerry.

"I want a toy."

Jerry saw a boat.

"I like this boat," said Jerry.

"I want this boat."

Jerry saw a ball.

"I like this ball," said Jerry.

"I want this ball."

Jerry saw a train.

A big red train!

"I like this train," said Jerry.

"I want this train."

"Oh, Father," said Jerry.

"I want the ball.

I want the boat.

I want the train."

Father looked at Jerry.

"You want the ball," he said.

"You want the boat.

You want the train.

You may have one toy, Jerry.

Just one toy."

Jerry looked at the ball.

He looked at the train.

He looked at the boat.

"One toy! One toy!" he said.

"Just one toy."

Jerry saw a big airplane.

"Oh, see this airplane," he said.

"I want this big airplane."

"Yes, Jerry," said Father.

"You may have this airplane.

This is a good airplane.

This airplane can fly."

Jerry looked so happy.

"Yes, yes," he said.

"This airplane can fly.

This is my airplane.

Look, Father, look.

See my airplane fly.

I like my big airplane.

See it fly! See it fly!"

Jip

One morning Jip ran away.

Alice did not see Jip go.

Jerry did not see Jip go.

Jip had a happy look.

And he ran away.

He ran away to play.

Jip saw a little kitten.

"Bow-wow, bow-wow!" said Jip.

"I want to play with you.

So here I come."

Up and away went the kitten.

She did not have a happy look.

She did not want to play.

Not with a puppy like Jip!

Jip saw a pretty red bird.

"Bow-wow, bow-wow!" said Jip.

"Do not fly away.

Come and play with me."

Up and away went the bird.

He had to fly away.

He did not want to play.

Not with a puppy like Jip!

Jip saw a little rabbit.

"Bow-wow, bow-wow!" said Jip.

Away went the rabbit.

Hop, hop! Hop, hop!

She came to a rabbit hole.

Down, down she went.

Jip came to the rabbit hole.

"Bow-wow, bow-wow!" he said.

"Come out, rabbit, come out!"

Little rabbit did not come out.

Jip saw a big, big duck.

"Bow-wow, bow-wow!" said Jip.

He ran at the big, big duck.

Away went the duck.

"See me fly," she said.

"See me fly away home.

I do not want to play.

Not with a puppy like you!"

Jip saw May, and May saw Jip.

"Jip, Jip, Jip!" said May.

"You ran away.

Alice looked and looked for you.

Jerry looked for you, too.

You come home.

You ride home with me."

So Jip went.

He did not have a happy look.

But he went home to Alice.

The New Coat

Alice had a little brown coat.

"My, oh, my," said Alice.

"This coat is pretty.

But it is too little for me.

Here is a big hole, too."

So Alice ran to Mother.

"See this big hole," she said.

"Yes," said Mother.

"This coat is too little for you.
I see a hole, too.
You may have a new coat, Alice."

"I want a red coat," said Alice.
"Please, Mother, please."

"Yes, Alice," said Mother.
"You may have a red coat."

So Mother went to the store.

Alice went to the store, too.

"Good morning," said the man.

"Good morning," said Mother.

"This is Alice.

She wants a new coat."

"I want a red coat," said Alice.

The man looked at the coats.

"I have a green coat," he said.

"Here is a pretty green coat."

"Yes," said Mother.

"This is a pretty green coat.
But Alice wants a red coat."

"Yes, yes," said Alice.

"I want a red coat."

Then the man looked and looked.

"I have a brown coat," he said.

"Here is a blue coat, too.

But I do not see a red coat."

"My, oh, my," said Alice.

"The green coat is pretty.

The brown coat is pretty.

The blue coat is pretty, too.

But I want a red coat."

COATS

Just then the man saw a box.

He looked in the box.

"Oh, Alice!" he said.

"Come here! Come here!"

Alice looked in the box, too.

"A red coat!" she said.

"Here is my red coat."

Then Alice laughed and laughed.

"Look, Alice," said the man.

"Here is a red cap, too."

"Oh, oh!" laughed Alice.

"See my red cap, Mother.

Do you like my new coat?

Do you like my new cap?

I do! I do!

See me, Mother, see me."

The Big, Big Puddle

Jerry ran to the window.

"Oh, see the rain," he said.

"Come to the window, Mother.

Come and see the rain."

Mother came to the window.

Down came the rain.

Down, down, down!

"Please, Mother," said Jerry.
"I want to play in the rain.
I want to jump in the puddles."
Jerry ran out in the rain.
He walked in the little puddles.
Splash, splash!
He walked in the big puddles.
Splash, splash, splash!

Alice ran to the window.

"Please, Mother," she said.

"I want to play in the rain, too."

Alice ran out in the rain.

She walked in the little puddles.

Splash, splash!

She walked in the big puddles.

Splash, splash, splash!

Jerry saw a big, big puddle.

"Come here, Alice," said Jerry.

"See this big, big puddle."

Alice ran to Jerry.

"My, oh, my!" said Alice.

"This puddle is too big for me."

"Come on, Alice," said Jerry.

"This puddle is not too big.

Come on! Come on!

One, two, three, jump!"

Jerry jumped
into the big, big puddle.

Alice jumped into the puddle, too.

Splash, splash, splash, splash!

"Here comes Jip," said Jerry.

"Look out, Alice, look out.

Jip is going to jump on you."

But Jip did not jump on Alice.

He jumped up on Jerry.

Down into the puddle went Jerry.

Splash, splash, splash, splash!

Alice laughed and laughed.

A Box for Alice

Mother had to go to the city.

"Jerry is going, too," she said.

"Please, Mother," said Alice.

"I want to go to the city.

I want to ride on the train."

"Not this morning," said Mother.

"You may go to play with May.

But you can not go to the city."

Alice did not look happy.

"I want to go," she said.

"I like to go to the city."

"What! What!" said Father.

"Is this Alice?

I like Alice.

But you do not look like Alice.

Alice is pretty.

You do not look pretty."

Alice looked at Father.

Then she laughed.

"My name IS Alice," she said.

"You like me and my name, too.

Good-by, Mother! Good-by, Jerry!"

Alice said good-by

with a happy look.

Then Mother and Jerry

went to the city.

Alice went to play with May.

Jip went with Alice.

May had a pretty play house.

She had three big dolls.

She had three little dolls, too.

She had toys and toys and toys.

Jip did not like toys.

He ran to play with Brown Puppy.

By and by Alice went home.

She saw Father at the window.

"Is Mother home?" she said.

"She is not here," said Father.

"The train did not come.

You may have something to eat.

Then you may look for Mother."

Alice had something good to eat.

Then she ran to look for Mother.

Alice looked up the walk.

She looked down the walk.

By and by she saw Mother.

"Here she comes," said Alice.

And away she ran to Mother.

"Look, Alice," said Mother.

"Here is a box I got in the city."

"What is in it?" said Alice.

"Something red," said Jerry.

"Something red for that new coat."

"Blue, too," said Mother.

"Something blue is in that box.

I got something green, Alice.

I got something brown, too."

"In one box?" said Alice.

"Red and blue and green and brown!
What is it? What is it?"

"Look and see," laughed Mother.

Then Alice looked.

"Oh!" she said with a happy look.

"This is just what I wanted.
Just what I wanted, Mother."

A Dog for Jerry

Jerry wanted a dog.
One day he ran to Father.

"Oh, Father," he said.
"I like Jip.
But Jip is just a puppy.
I want a good big dog."

"What! What!" said Father.
"Two dogs in one house!
I can not have that."

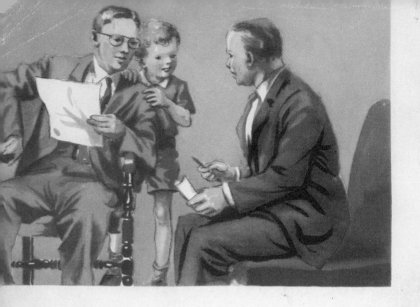

Days and days went by.

Jerry did not have a dog.

"A boy wants a dog," said Jerry.

"A boy wants a good big dog."

One day a man came to see Father.

The man looked at Jerry.

"Do you like dogs?" he said.

"Yes, I do," said Jerry.

"I like good big dogs."

"I have a big dog," said the man.
"And I have to go to the city.
I have to stay for days and days.
My dog can not go to the city.
Mac is not a city dog.
I want a good home for Mac.
A good home with a good boy!"

"Here is that boy," said Jerry.
"That dog can stay with me."

"What! What!" said Father.
"Two dogs in one house!
Mother will not like that."

The man looked at Father.

"Mac is a good dog," he said.
"I will come home again.
I will not stay in the city.
Then Mac can come home, too."

"Yes," said Father. "I see.
But Mother will not like that dog."

"Yes, she will," said Jerry.

And he ran to look for Mother.

"Please, Mother, please," he said.
"Mac can not go to the city.
Mac is not a city dog."

He said this again and again.

By and by Mother said, "Yes!
That dog may come, Jerry.
But he can not stay in this house."

One day went by.

Then Mac came to stay with Jerry.

He was a big dog and a good dog.

He had a house in the garden.

Jerry was happy,

and Mac was happy, too.

"You see, Mother," said Jerry.

"A boy likes a big dog.

A big dog with a name like Mac!"

SURPRISE

Something for Mother

Mother had a garden.

"Oh, Mother," said Alice.

"I want a garden.

A little garden, just for me."

"Come with me," said Mother.

Alice went with Mother.

By and by she had a garden.

A little garden, just for Alice!

One day Jip ran into the garden.
By and by Alice saw a hole.
A big, big hole!
Jip was down in the hole.
"Get out, get out!" said Alice.
"And stay out, too.
I do not want holes in my garden."
Away ran Jip.

One day the rain came.

Down, down, down it came.

Alice saw rain puddles
in the little brown garden.

Two days and three days went by.

"Oh, Mother!" said Alice.

"Come and see! Come and see!

My garden is not brown.

I have a pretty green garden."

Mother came to see the garden.

A little brown rabbit came, too.

"Hop away, rabbit," said Alice.

"And stay away, too.

I do not want you in my garden."

Hop, hop, hop went the rabbit.

Mother and Alice walked away.

Then Brown Rabbit came again

to the pretty green garden.

The days went by and by.
One morning Alice ran
into the garden.

"Oh, look, look," she said.
"I see something blue.
Here, and here, and here!
Mother likes blue.
Here is something she will like.
Here in my garden!"

Alice got something blue.
She got something green, too.
Then she ran to Mother.

"Surprise! Surprise!" said Alice.
"Here is something green.
And something blue.
Something pretty, just for you."

"Oh, Alice," said Mother.
"I like blue, and I like surprises.
I like surprises just for me."

A Good Wish

One morning Jerry ran to Mother.

"Do you like to wish?" he said.

"I do.

I wish I had a big airplane.

Not a toy airplane!

A big airplane to fly in!"

Mother laughed.

"You may wish and wish," she said.

"But you will not get that wish.

Not this morning!"

"I want a new name," said Jerry.

"I wish I had the name Jack.

Jack is a good name for a boy.

Father likes that name, too."

"What! What!" said Mother.
"You want a new name!
I like the name Jerry.
You can not have that wish."

Then Mother said, "I will wish.
I wish I had a boy
to go to the store for me."
"Oh," said Jerry.
"You may have that wish.
Alice and I will go, Mother."
So Alice said good-by.
And Jerry said good-by.
Then Alice and Jerry went
to the store.

Jerry saw a little brown pony.

He saw a boy, too.

"Oh, look, Alice," said Jerry.

"That boy is going for a ride.

I wish I had a pony.

A little brown pony to ride."

"So do I," said Alice.

"But you can wish and wish.

And you will not get that wish."

Alice and Jerry came
to the store.

"I wish I had a store,"
said Alice.
"Not this store!
I wish I had a toy store.
A store with dolls and balls
and boats and trains.
I want toys and toys and toys."

But Alice did not get that wish.

"I wish I had a store,"
said Jerry.
"Just a little store!
I want rabbits that hop
and birds that fly.
I want ducks and kittens,
and dogs like Mac.
I will have puppy dogs, too."

But Jerry did not get that wish.

61

Jerry got what Mother wanted
at the store.

Then Alice and Jerry ran home.

"Oh, Mother," said Jerry.

"I wish I had something to eat.
Something good!"

"So do I," said Alice.

"Here it is," said Mother.

"Here is something you like."

"Surprise! Surprise!" said Jerry.

"I got my wish."

"Surprise! Surprise!" said Alice.

"I got my wish, too."

Can You Find Alice?

Mother came to the window.

"Oh, Jerry," she said.

"Please find Alice.

Here is her red coat.

Here is her red cap.

But I can not find Alice."

"I can find her," said Jerry.

And away he went.

"Alice! Alice!" said Jerry.

But Alice did not come.

Just then Jerry saw a box.

He saw a red train, too.

"Alice had this box," he said.

"She had my red train, too.

Alice was here.

But she is not here now."

Then Jerry saw Jack.

Jack had a new blue boat.

"Did you see Alice?" said Jerry.

"Alice was here," said Jack.

"She came to play with me.

But she is not here now."

"Come with me," said Jerry.

"I want to find Alice."

Jack ran into a big rain puddle.

Splash! Splash! Splash!

He got the new blue boat.

Then he ran on with Jerry.

Jack and Jerry saw a toy store.

"Alice is here," said Jerry.

"She likes this toy store man."

So Jack and Jerry walked in.

"Did you see Alice?" said Jerry.

"Alice was here," said the man.

"I saw her at the window.

But she did not come in.

And she is not here now."

Jerry and Jack walked on.

Jip ran and jumped on Jerry.

"Get down, Jip," said Jerry.

"Go and find Alice. Go, Jip, go!"

"Bow-wow, bow-wow!" said Jip.

He wanted to say, "I can find her.

Just see me go."

Away went the puppy.

Away went Jack and Jerry.

"Oh, look, Jack," said Jerry.

"Jip is going home.

That puppy is just going home.

He can not find Alice."

"Do not say that," said Jack.

"Jip is a good puppy.

You and I can not find Alice.

But Jip can. Here she is!"

Alice was at home again.
What a surprise for Jerry!

"Mother wants you," he said.

"Is she going away?" said Alice.
"Is she going to the city?"

"Come and see," said Jerry.
"Good-by, Jack, good-by."

"Good-by, good-by," said Jack.

Then Alice and Jerry ran
into the house.
Jack ran home to play
with that new blue boat.

A Walk with Mother

One morning Mother said,
"Come with me, Alice and Jerry.
Do you like surprises?"
"Yes, yes," said Jerry.
"I like surprises."
"So do I," said Alice.
"What is the surprise?"
"Come and see," said Mother.
Mother walked and walked.
Alice and Jerry walked with her.
"I like surprises," said Alice.
"But I do not like
to walk and walk and walk.
I want the surprise now."

"Please, Mother," said Jerry.

"I want the surprise, too."

"Come on," laughed Mother.

"This is a good surprise.

It is little and brown.

You can ride on it."

A brown kitten ran up to Alice.

"Mew, mew, mew!" it said.

It wanted to say, "Come and play.

I want to play this morning."

"Oh, oh!" said Alice.

"This kitten is little.

It is brown, too.

But this is not the surprise.

I can not ride on a kitten."

A brown dog ran up to Jerry.

He was a big dog like Mac.

"Bow-wow, bow-wow!" said the dog.

"Go away! Go away!" said Jerry.

"This dog is not the surprise.

He is brown.

But I can not ride on a dog."

Mother and Alice and Jerry

walked on.

By and by Mother came to a house.

It was a pretty red house.

"The surprise is here," she said.

A man came out to see Mother.

"So this is Alice," he said.

"And this is Jerry.

Come with me, Alice and Jerry.

I have something you want to see."

"What is it?" said Jerry.

"What is it?" said Alice.

"Come and see," laughed the man.

Just then Jerry saw something.

He saw something little and brown.

"A pony! A pony!" he said.

"I want a ride."

"A pony! A pony!" said Alice.

"I want a ride, too."

"Jump on, jump on," said the man.

"Jump on and have a good ride.

One, two, three! Up you go."

Away went the brown pony.

Away went Alice and Jerry.

Jerry was so happy.

"Oh, Mother," he said.

"I like surprises like this.

One day I saw a boy and a pony.

I wanted a ride.

But I did not get a ride.

Now I can ride and ride and ride."

"Yes, yes," said Alice.

"I want to ride and ride, too."

ANIMALS

Little Goat

Little Goat ran away.

He ran and ran and ran.

By and by Little Goat stopped.

"I like to eat," he said.

"I will find something to eat.

I will eat and eat and eat."

What did Little Goat see?

He saw a cap, a big brown cap.

"Here is something to eat,"
he said.

"I can eat caps.

I like to eat caps."

And Little Goat ate and ate.
Then he ran on.

What did Little Goat see?

He saw a doll, a little old doll.

Little Goat stopped.

"Here is something to eat,"
he said.

"I can eat dolls.

I can eat a little old doll."

And Little Goat ate and ate.

What did Little Goat see?

He saw a ball, a big, big ball.

Little Goat stopped again.

"Here is something to eat,"
he said.

"I can eat balls.

I like to eat balls."

And Little Goat ate and ate.

What did Little Goat see?

He saw a kitten.

The kitten looked like a ball.

"Here is something to eat,"
he said.

"I can eat little balls.

I can eat big balls."

And Little Goat started to eat.

Up jumped the little kitten.

"Mew, mew! Go away!" she said.

"I am not a ball.

I am a kitten. Mew, mew, mew!"

"What? What?" said Little Goat.

"You are a kitten.

You are not a ball.

I can not eat kittens.

So I will not eat you."

Then Little Goat started for home.

The Little Duck

The little duck went for a walk.
He saw a kitten.

The kitten said, "Mew, mew!"

The little duck stopped.

"What pretty talk that is!"
said the little duck.

"I wish I could talk like that."

But he could not say, "Mew, mew!"

The little duck saw a hen.

The hen said, "Cluck, cluck!"

The little duck stopped.

"What pretty talk that is!"
said the little duck.

"I wish I could talk like that."

But he could not say,
"Cluck, cluck!"

The little duck saw a bird.

The bird said, "Tweet, tweet!"

The little duck stopped.

"What pretty talk that is!"
said the little duck.

"I wish I could talk like that."

But he could not say,

"Tweet, tweet!"

The little duck saw a rooster.

The rooster said,

"Cock-a-doodle-doo!"

The little duck stopped.

"What pretty talk that is!"
said the little duck.

"I wish I could talk like that."

But he could not say,

"Cock-a-doodle-doo!"

The little duck went on.

"I can not talk like the hen,"
he said.

"I can not talk like the kitten.

I can not talk like the bird.

I can not talk like the rooster."

The little duck looked up.

He saw Mother Duck.

Mother Duck said, "Quack, quack!"

The little duck stopped.

"What pretty talk that is!"
said the little duck.

"I can talk just like that."

And he did.

"Quack, quack! Quack, quack!"

Little Jack Rabbit

Mother Rabbit lived in a nest.
Three little rabbits
lived in the nest, too.

Little Jack Rabbit was not happy.
He did not like the nest.

"I want to go away," he said.

But Mother Rabbit said,

"You are too little to go away."

One day Mother Rabbit went away.

Then Jack Rabbit said,

"I will not stay in this nest.

I can run away,

and I will run away.

I am a big Jack Rabbit."

Hop, hop, hop he went.

He came to a big garden.

"I am so big,"
said little Jack Rabbit.
"I like to hop.
I like to play.
I am too big to stay
in a nest all day.
I will play in this pretty garden."
Jack Rabbit ran into the garden.
Two white rabbits lived
in a house in the garden.

Jack Rabbit looked
at the two white rabbits.

"My coat is brown," he said.
"You have white coats.
But you are rabbits, too.
And I will play with you."

So Jack Rabbit played
with the two white rabbits.
The three rabbits
played and played all the morning.

The garden gate was open.
By and by something big
ran in at the open gate.

"Bow-wow, bow-wow!" it said.
Now the rabbits did not play.

"Here comes a dog,"
said the two white rabbits.
"Run, Jack Rabbit, run!
That dog will eat you."

Away ran the two white rabbits.
Away to the little house!

But Jack Rabbit
did not have a house.
He lived in a nest.
And he could not find his nest.
So he ran on and on.

By and by Jack Rabbit stopped.
He could not see the dog.
He could not find his nest.
He could not find his mother.
He was just a little rabbit.
And he wanted his mother.

Night came.

Little Jack Rabbit

did not like the night.

He wanted to find his mother.

By and by he saw something.

It came hop, hop, hop.

It was big.

It had a brown coat.

It was Mother Rabbit.

What a surprise

for little Jack Rabbit!

Mother Rabbit looked
at her little rabbit.

"You ran away," she said.
"I have looked and looked for you.
Come home with me, Jack Rabbit.
You are too little to run away."

The two rabbits started for home.
Now little Jack Rabbit was happy.

"I can run home.
And I will run home.
I will stay in my nest,"
said little Jack Rabbit.

A Good Breakfast

The little pig ran away.
He came to a garden.
The garden gate was open.
So the little pig looked in.

"I see a good breakfast,"
said the little pig.

He went into the garden
and started to eat.

The white hen came by.

She stopped at the open gate.

"Cluck, cluck!" said the hen.

"I see a good breakfast."

"Wee, wee, wee! Come in!"
said the little pig.

The white hen went
into the garden.

She started to eat breakfast, too.

The red cow came by.

She stopped at the open gate.

"Moo, moo! Moo, moo!" she said.

"I see a good breakfast."

"Cluck, cluck! Come in!"
said the white hen.

The red cow went
into the garden.

She started to eat breakfast, too.

The brown pony came by.

He stopped at the open gate.

"I see a good breakfast,"
said the brown pony.

"Moo, moo! Come in!"
said the red cow.

The brown pony went
into the garden.

He started to eat breakfast, too.

A man came to the open gate.

He saw the little pig.

He saw the white hen.

He saw the red cow.

He saw the brown pony.

"Get out! Get out!" he said.

"Go home to the barnyard.

And stay in that barnyard, too."

The little pig ran.

The white hen ran.

The red cow ran.

The brown pony ran.

All the animals started
to run home to the barnyard.

"I had a good breakfast,"
said the little pig.

"I want to come again,"
said the brown pony.

"I will come again,"
said the white hen.

"I will, too," said the red cow.

The animals went to the garden
again and again and again.

But the gate was not open.

BETSY LEE

The New Doll

One morning
Alice ate her breakfast.
Then she ran out to play.

A man stopped at the gate.
He had a big box.

"This box is for Alice White,"
said the man.

"My, oh, my!" said Alice.
"I am Alice White.
This big box is for me."

Alice ran to find Mother.

"This box is for me," she said.

"So I will open it.

My, oh, my! A new doll!

This is just what I wanted."

The new doll was big.

It was very, very pretty.

It had a pretty blue coat.

It had a pretty blue cap.

The cap had

a red and white airplane on it.

Alice played with her new doll.

"Oh, Mother," said Alice.

"My new doll is very, very pretty.

I will name my doll Betsy.

But I have two names.

My name is Alice White.

My doll can have two names.

I will name her Betsy Lee."

"That is a good name,"
said Mother.

Alice looked at Betsy Lee.

"My, oh, my," she said.

"You are so pretty, Betsy Lee.

I wish you could talk to me."

But Betsy Lee did not say a word.

"I like you, Betsy Lee.

Do you like me?" said Alice.

But Betsy Lee did not say a word.

In the Garden

By and by Alice said,
"I will not stay in the house.
I want to play in the garden.

    Come, Betsy Lee!

    Come, walk with me!

My, oh, my! I like to say that.
I will say it again.

    Come, Betsy Lee!

    Come, walk with me!"

Alice went into the garden
with her new doll.

Mother Rabbit lived in the garden.

"Mother Rabbit," said Alice.

"You have a brown coat.

Do you see Betsy Lee?

Her coat is so blue."

Mother Rabbit looked at Betsy Lee.

Then she gave a big hop.

She gave one big hop and ran away.

"Mother Rabbit did not like you,"
said Alice.

"But I like you, Betsy Lee."

"Tweet! Tweet! Tweet! Tweet!"
said a little brown bird.
He lived in the garden, too.

Alice walked to the garden gate.
"Little Brown Bird," she said.
"You can talk to me.
You can fly, too."

Away went Brown Bird to his nest.
Then Alice looked at Betsy Lee.
"What can you do?" she said.
But Betsy Lee did not say a word.

In the Barnyard

Then Alice said again,
"Come, Betsy Lee!
Come, walk with me!"
Alice went into the barnyard
with Betsy Lee.
Red Rooster lived in the barnyard.
He started to talk to Alice.
"Cock-a-doodle-doo!" he said.
"Red Rooster can say,
'Cock-a-doodle-doo,'" said Alice.
"I wish you could talk, Betsy Lee."

Red Cow lived in the barnyard.

She looked at Alice and Betsy Lee.

Red Cow was very old.

"Red Cow," said Alice.

"You are very, very old.

You are not very pretty.

But you can talk to me."

"Moo, moo!" said the red cow.

"Moo, moo, moo, moo!"

Betsy Lee looked at the red cow.

But Betsy Lee did not say a word.

All the white hens
walked up to Alice.

"Here is something
for you to eat," said Alice.

The white hens ate and ate.

"Cluck, cluck, cluck, cluck!"
said all the hens.

"The white hens can say,
'Cluck, cluck,'" said Alice.
"What can you say, Betsy Lee?"

But Betsy Lee did not say a word.

All the ducks started
to talk to Alice.

"Quack, quack, quack, quack!"
The big ducks said it.
The little ducks said it.
All the ducks said it.
"Quack, quack, quack, quack!"

Betsy Lee walked on with Alice.
But Betsy Lee did not say a word.

Then the little pigs
started to talk to Alice.

"Wee, wee, wee, wee!"
said all the little pigs.

Alice laughed and laughed.

"Little pigs," she said.
"You like to eat and eat and eat.
But you can talk to me."

"Wee, wee, wee!" said the pigs.

But Betsy Lee did not say a word.

Then Alice saw a big white goat.

The barnyard gate was open.

The goat ran into the barnyard.

Away went all the hens.

Away went all the little pigs.

Away went all the ducks.

Away went the big red rooster.

But the red cow did not run.

She lived in that barnyard,

and she could not run.

She was too old.

"Come, Betsy Lee, come!"
said Alice.
"I am going to run home.
I do not like that goat.
All he can do is
eat and eat and eat.
He may want to eat you.
I am going to run home."

So Alice and Betsy Lee ran home.

Betsy Lee Talks

Alice looked at Betsy Lee.

"You are so pretty," she said.

"I like this blue coat.

I like this blue cap.

I like the red and white airplane.

I like you, Betsy Lee.

You are my doll.

But oh, I wish you could talk!"

"All the animals can talk to me.

The red rooster can say,

'Cock-a-doodle-doo.'

The white hens can say,

'Cluck, cluck.'

The old red cow can say, 'Moo, moo.'

All the little pigs can say,

'Wee, wee, wee, wee.'

The ducks can say, 'Quack, quack.'

You can not say a word.

But I like you, Betsy Lee."

That night Alice said again,

"I wish you could talk, Betsy Lee."

Then she gave Betsy Lee a big hug.

"Ma-ma! Ma-ma!" said Betsy Lee.

"Oh, oh! Betsy Lee!" said Alice.

"You can talk! You can talk!"

She gave Betsy Lee a big, big hug.

One, two, three big hugs!

"Ma-ma! Ma-ma!" said Betsy Lee.

"Ma-ma! Ma-ma! Ma-ma! Ma-ma!"

MR. CARL and JACK

My Little Girl

Alice lived
in a pretty white house.
Mr. Carl lived
in a white house, too.

Mr. Carl was old.

Yes, he was very, very old.

He liked Alice,

and Alice liked Mr. Carl.

"Alice is my little girl,"

Mr. Carl said again and again.

Mr. Carl liked birds, too.

He had birds and birds and birds

in his white house.

Red birds!

Blue birds!

Brown birds!

Alice liked to look

at all the birds.

One morning
Alice ate her breakfast.
Then she went for a walk
with Betsy Lee.

She saw Mr. Carl in his garden.
So she stopped to say hello.

"Do you like birds, Betsy Lee?
I do," said Alice.

"Ma-ma! Ma-ma!" said Betsy Lee.

"Here comes my little girl,"
said old Mr. Carl.

"Hello, Alice! Hello, Betsy Lee!
Come into the house with me.
My birds want to see you."

So Alice and Betsy Lee
went into the house with Mr. Carl.

All the birds said,
"Tweet! Tweet! Tweet!"
The red birds said it.
The blue birds said it.
The brown birds said it.
"Tweet! Tweet!" for Alice.
And "Tweet!" for Betsy Lee.

"Oh, Mr. Carl," said Alice.
"The birds are so pretty.
And look, Mr. Carl, look!
The birds want something to eat."

So Alice gave the red birds
something to eat.
She gave the blue birds
something to eat.
She gave the brown birds
something to eat, too.

"Tweet! Tweet! Tweet!"
said all the birds.
"Tweet! Tweet!" for Alice.
And "Tweet!" for Betsy Lee.

The Big Green Bird

"Now the birds are happy,"
said Alice.
"I gave all the birds
something to eat."

"Not all the birds,"
laughed old Mr. Carl.
"I have one new bird, Alice.
And you can not find that bird."

"Yes, I can," said Alice.
She looked and looked and looked.

"Look again! Look again!"
laughed old Mr. Carl.

Alice looked again.

But she could not find that bird.

"Help me, Mr. Carl," she said.

"Help me find it! Please! Please!"

Mr. Carl got up

and walked to the open window.

"Here you are, Alice," he said.

Just then something said,

"Hello, Alice! Hello, little girl!"

What was it? What was it?

Alice ran to the open window.

She saw a bird, a big green bird.

And it said,

"Hello, Alice! Hello, little girl!"

Alice laughed and laughed.

"Oh! Oh!" said Alice.
"A bird that can talk!
A bird that can say my name!
Look, Betsy Lee, look!"

Alice gave Betsy Lee a big hug.
"Ma-ma! Ma-ma!" said Betsy Lee.

Then Alice gave the green bird
something to eat.
But the green bird did not say,
"Tweet! Tweet!"
It said,
"Hello, Alice! Hello, little girl!"

And Alice laughed and laughed.

The Best Store

Jack liked stores.

He liked stores that had toys.

He liked stores
that had something good to eat.

He liked stores
that had caps and coats.

But the store he liked best
was the animal store.

In the morning Jack liked
to eat his breakfast.
Then he liked to run down
to the animal store.
What did he see in the window?

One day he saw rabbits.
Big rabbits and little rabbits
with pretty white coats.

One day he saw kittens.
Three little kittens
that played with a big red ball.

One day he saw a dog.
A little brown and white dog!
Just the dog that Jack wanted!

"Hello, little dog," said Jack.

The little dog jumped up
on the window to look at Jack.

"Good puppy! Good puppy!"
said Jack.

"You are just the dog I want.
I wish I could have you
for my little dog."

"Bow-wow! Bow-wow!" said the dog.
He wanted to say, "I wish so, too."

One day, two days, three days
that dog was in the window.
Jack came to the window
again and again and again.
Mr. Green was the man
in the animal store.

For three days Mr. Green
saw Jack at his window.
So by and by he said,

"Come in, Jack, come in.
Do you like that little dog?"

"Yes, I do," said Jack.
"He is the best dog in this store.
What is his name?"

"His name is Snap,"
laughed Mr. Green.
"But he is not my best dog.
He snaps at my rabbits.
He snaps at my birds.
He snaps at all my animals."

"He will not snap at me,"
said Jack.

"I will open the window and see,"
said Mr. Green.

Out jumped the little puppy.
He ran up to Jack.

Jack gave the puppy a big hug.
The little dog did not snap.
He jumped up on Jack
and started to play.

"Snap likes you, Jack,"
said Mr. Green.

Then Jack and the puppy
played and played and played.

By and by Mr. Green said,
"Jump into the window, Snap."
But Snap did not jump.

Then Jack said, "Good dog!
Jump into the window, Snap."
And Snap jumped.

Mr. Green looked at Jack.

"You like animals," he said.
"And I like you.
I want a boy to help me
in my store.
Are you the boy to help me?"

"Yes, I am," said Jack.
"I am the boy to help you.
I will stay and help you now."

"Good!" said Mr. Green.

So Jack gave all the animals
something good to eat.
He gave Snap something
very, very good.

"You are the best animal
in this store," he said.
And he gave Snap a big hug.

By and by Mr. Green said,

"That is all for now, Jack.

You are a good help.

Come again in the morning."

So Jack said, "Good-by, Snap.

Good-by, Mr. Green."

Then he started for home.

He saw Alice and Jerry

on the walk by his house.

"I saw the best dog," said Jack.

"Not the best dog," said Jerry.

"Mac is the best dog."

"Jip is the best," said Alice.

"He is, too! He is, too!"

"Snap is the best dog," said Jack.

"He is! He is! He is!"

Then Jack ran into the house
to talk to his mother.

A Dog for Jack

Day in and day out
Jack came to the store.
Day in and day out
he came to help Mr. Green.
Now and then he played with Snap.

Then one day Mr. Green said,
"Snap is too big to stay
in this window now.
He wants a home.
Can you help me out, Jack?
May Snap go home with you?"

"Home with me!" said Jack.

"Home with me to stay!"

"Yes," laughed Mr. Green.

"Home with you to stay!"

Jack was so happy.

He could not say a word.

He just looked at Mr. Green.

Mr. Green walked to the window.

One, two, three,

and the window was open.

"Jump out, Snap," said Mr. Green.

Out jumped the little dog.

He ran and jumped on Jack.

Jack gave Snap a big, big hug.

"Now you are my little dog,"
he said.

"But you did not snap at me.

Snap is not a good name

for a dog like you.

I will find you a good name."

And Jack did.

GOOD NIGHT

A Happy Day

Alice and Jerry had a happy day.

Jerry got up and ate
his breakfast.

Then he said,
"I am going to help Jack.
I am going to help Jack get
a new name for his dog Snap."

So Jerry ran to find Jack.
The two boys played and played
all the morning.

Alice had something she liked
for breakfast.

"This is the best breakfast,"
she said.

Then she ran to say hello
to old Mr. Carl.

"Here comes my little girl,"
said old Mr. Carl.

The big green bird said,
"Hello, Alice! Hello, little girl!"

By and by Alice and Jerry
came home again.
Then Mother and Alice and Jerry
went for a boat ride.

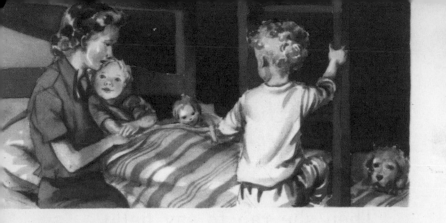

Good Night

Now it was night.
Mother came to say good night
to Alice and Jerry.
She gave Alice a big hug.
She gave Jerry a big hug, too.

"Good night, Mother," said Alice.
"I have had the best day."

"So have I," said Jerry.
"Good night, Mother, good night."

Then Mother went away.

By and by Alice said,

"Jerry! Jerry! I want to play.

Animals in the barnyard!

That is what I want to play."

"Good!" said Jerry. "Here I go!"

So Jerry started.

"I want a barnyard," said Jerry.

"In my barnyard I will have—

A big red rooster to say,

'Cock-a-doodle-doo.'"

"I want a barnyard," said Alice.
"In my barnyard I will have—
A big red rooster to say,
'Cock-a-doodle-doo.'
And one brown pony for me to ride."

"I want a barnyard," said Jerry.
"In my barnyard I will have—
A big red rooster to say,
'Cock-a-doodle-doo.'
One brown pony for me to ride.
And big ducks and little ducks
to splash in the rain puddles."

"I want a barnyard," said Alice.
"In my barnyard I will have—
A big red rooster to say,
'Cock-a-doodle-doo.'
One brown pony for me to ride.
Big ducks and little ducks
to splash in the rain puddles.
And big pigs and little pigs
that eat and eat and eat."

"I want a barnyard," said Jerry.
"In my barnyard I will have—
A big red rooster to say,
'Cock-a-doodle-doo.'
One brown pony for me to ride!
Big ducks and little ducks
to splash in the rain puddles!
Big pigs and little pigs
that eat and eat and eat!
And a big mother hen to stay
on her nest and cluck."

"I want a barnyard," said Alice.
"In my barnyard I will have—
A big red rooster to say,
'Cock-a-doodle-doo.'
One brown pony for me to ride!
Big ducks and little ducks
to splash in the rain puddles!
Big pigs and little pigs
that eat and eat and eat!
A big mother hen to stay
on her nest and cluck!
And three old white goats
to run at all the animals!"

Just then Mother came in.

"Now, see here," she said.

"I do not want a barnyard.

I want a house with one little boy
and one little girl.

I want that little boy
and that little girl
to say, 'Good night.'

And then do not say a word."

Alice laughed, and Jerry laughed.

Then Alice gave Mother a big hug.

"This little girl will not
say a word," she said.

"Good night, Mother, good night."

Jerry gave Mother a big hug.

"Good night, Mother," he said.

Then Alice did not say a word.

And Jerry did not say a word.

Not one word!

Acknowledgments

Grateful acknowledgment is made for permission to make adaptations from copyrighted material as follows:

"Surprise" from "Happy House" by Zillah K. Macdonald.

"The Little Duck" from "Little Duckling Tries His Voice" by Marjorie M. LaFleur in *Child Life*, published by Rand McNally and Company.

"A Good Breakfast" from "The Little Pig" by Maud Lindsay in *More Mother Stories*, published by Milton Bradley Company.

Word List

The following list includes all the 78 words introduced and developed in the *Preprimers*. They are all repeated in the first unit of this *Basic Primer*. Each number refers to the *Primer* page on which the word first appears.

a, 7
airplane, 14
Alice, 5
and, 5
at, 13

big, 11
blue, 26
boat, 10
brown, 6

can, 14
cap, 28
come, 6

did, 16
do, 18
down, 7

Father, 10

go, 16
going, 34
good, 14

good-by, 37
got, 40
green, 25

had, 16
have, 13
he, 13
here, 6
home, 20
house, 38

I, 6
in, 27
is, 14
it, 15

Jerry, 5
Jip, 16
jump, 30

kitten, 17

like, 10

little, 6
look, 7
looked, 7

man, 24
may, 13
me, 18
morning, 16
Mother, 22
my, 15

name, 37
not, 16

on, 33
one, 13

play, 16
pretty, 18
puppy, 17

ran, 8
red, 11
ride, 21

said, 6
saw, 7
see, 6
she, 7
something, 6
store, 24

the, 8
this, 10
three, 33
to, 16
too, 8
train, 11
two, 33

up, 17

walked, 30
want, 10
went, 8
what, 36
window, 29
with, 17

yes, 14
you, 13

Word List

The following list includes the 102 words in this *Primer* that were not introduced and developed in the four *Preprimers*.

Presentation Unit

5

6 Rabbit

7 oh

8 hop

9 hole

10 toys

11 ball

12

13 just

14 fly

15 so
happy

16 away

17 bow-wow

18 bird

19 came
out

20 duck

21 for
but

22 new
coat

23 please

24

25

26 then

27 box
laughed

28

29 puddle
rain

30 splash

31

32

33 jumped
into

34

35 city

36

37

38 dolls

39 by
eat

40 walk

41 that

42 wanted

43 dog
day

44 boy

45 stay
Mac

46 will
again

47

48 was
garden

Absorption Unit

49 surprise

50

51 get

52

53

54

55

56 wish
Jack

57

58

59 pony

60

61

62

63 find
her

64 now

65

66

67 say

68

69

70

71

72 mew

159

73

74

75

76

Presentation Unit

77 animals

78 Goat stopped

79 ate

80 old

81

82 started

83 am are

84 talk could

85 hen cluck

86 tweet

87 rooster cock-a-doodle-doo

88

89 quack

90 lived nest

91 run

92 all white

93 played

94 gate open

95 his

96 night

97

98 breakfast pig

99 wee

100 cow moo

101

102 barnyard

103

104

Absorption Unit

105 Betsy Lee

106

107 very

108

109 word

110

111 gave

112

113

114

115

116

117

118

119

120

121

122 hug Ma-ma

Presentation Unit

123 Mr. Carl

124 girl

125 liked

126 hello

127

128

129

130

131 help

132

133

134 best

135

136

137

138 Snap

139

140

141

142

143

144

145

146

Absorption Unit

147

148

149

150

151

152

153

154

155

156

157